j

Choose Your Own Adventure #48

SKYLARK

"I DON
ADVEN
says Jes
kids bet
choose
what ki
Choose

"These
can picl
the story

"I love f

"I like

"A six-y
making

Bantam Skylark Books in the Choose Your Own Adventure®
Series
Ask your bookseller for the books you have missed

YOU ARE INVISIBLE

BY SUSAN SAUNDERS

ILLUSTRATED BY RON WING

An Edward Packard Book

A BANTAM SKYLARK BOOK®
TORONTO · NEW YORK · LONDON · SYDNEY · AUCKLAND

RL 2, 007–009

YOU ARE INVISIBLE
A Bantam Skylark Book / February 1989

*CHOOSE YOUR OWN ADVENTURE® is a registered trademark of
Bantam Books, a division of Bantam Doubleday Dell Publishing Group, Inc.
Original conception of Edward Packard.
Skylark Books is a registered trademark of Bantam Books, a division of
Bantam Doubleday Dell Publishing Group, Inc.
Registered in U.S. Patent and Trademark Office and elsewhere.*

*Interior art by Ron Wing
Cover art by Bill Schmidt*

ISBN 0-553-15685-3

Published simultaneously in the United States and Canada

Bantam Books are published by Bantam Books, a division of Bantam Doubleday Dell Publishing Group, Inc. Its trademark, consisting of the
words "Bantam Books" and the portrayal of a rooster, is Registered in U.S.
Patent and Trademark Office and in other countries. Marca Registrada.
Bantam Books, 666 Fifth Avenue, New York, New York 10103.

PRINTED IN THE UNITED STATES OF AMERICA

CW   0 9 8 7 6 5 4 3 2 1

YOU ARE INVISIBLE

READ THIS FIRST!!!

Most books are about other people.

This book is about you—and the adventures you have when you become invisible.

Do not read this book from the first page through to the last page. Instead, start at page one and read until you come to your first choice. Decide what you want to do. Then turn to the page shown and see what happens next.

When you come to the end of a story, go back and try another choice. Every choice leads to a new adventure.

Good luck!

You and your family have just moved into a **1** big old house. It will take a lot of work to get the place into shape. Today you and your friend Robert are clearing out the attic. You are looking through old newspapers, mysterious boxes, and some rusty tin trunks.

You open a trunk. It's filled with strange-looking clothing: a shiny beaded dress, a checkered vest, and a long cape with a hood. The cape looks gray, but when you pull it out of the trunk, it shimmers with all the colors of the rainbow.

You put the cape on. It covers you from the top of your head to the tip of your toes. But it's so light you barely feel it.

You walk over to a cracked mirror in the corner of the attic to take a look at yourself.

Turn to page 2.

2   You peer into the mirror. But you don't see a thing! Your arms are missing, and so are your feet and legs. In fact, you don't see any of you—or the old cape, either.

"Where are you?" Robert calls out. "I'm not going to do all this work by myself."

But he's looking right at you! Is he joking . . . *or could you be invisible?*

Should you tell Robert about this magical cape? Or do you want to keep it a secret for now?

If you tell Robert about the cape, turn to page 12.

If you decide to sneak out without saying anything to him, turn to page 22.

4   You decide to find out what's going on down the street. You leave the ball game and race toward the shouting.

As you run, you hear a crash and more angry shouts. "You broke my windows! I'll get you for this!"

You turn onto Main Street and see a big kid

running up the sidewalk toward you. It's Larry. He's a bully, and he's always picking on you and your friends.

Mr. Brown, the butcher, is chasing Larry. So are Fred, the barber, and Mrs. Willis, the librarian.

Turn to page 9.

6   You don't want to give up the cape, but you don't want to fight with Robert either. "All right, we'll cut it in half," you say at last.

You find some scissors. Robert folds the cape over and cuts it right down the middle.

The cape was roomy, so each half is still very large. Robert wraps his half around himself. You hear him thumping down the stairs. Then you hear the front door slam shut. Quickly you put on your half of the cape and race after him. You want to find out what Robert is going to do.

You follow the sound of his steps. Sometimes you can actually *see* him! Not in the sunlight—it shines right through Robert and the cape. But you can just make him out in the shadows—a dim gray shape hurrying down the sidewalk!

Turn to page 43.

8   You've heard what happens to kids who sneak in. They have to sweep the whole lobby! You start to giggle. You can't wait to see Robert pushing a broom.

But you giggle too soon. You forget . . . the usher can see *you*, too!

The End

Larry's almost twice as big as you are! **9**
Should you try to stop him by tripping him?
Maybe if you barked and growled like a mean
dog you could scare him into stopping.

If you try to trip Larry, turn to page 33.

If you growl and bark like a mean dog,
turn to page 50.

10   You decide to stay out of the way, and you duck behind the big bush near the street.

Larry steps through the front door, and . . . *splat!* A water balloon explodes in his face!

Before Larry can react . . . *splat!* Another water balloon hits him. *Splat!* And another!

Suddenly you sneeze, "Ah-ah-*choooo!*"

"Come out of that bush, you little jerk!" Larry roars, wiping his dripping face. He thinks you tossed the balloons!

"You—you'd b-better watch it," you stammer. "I'm trained in karate!"

"Don't make me laugh!" Larry growls, stomping toward you, dripping wet.

Turn to page 52.

12   "I'm right here!" you say to Robert, taking off the cape.

Robert is speechless when you appear in front of him.

"It's this cape," you explain. "Now you see me . . ." You slip the cape on again. "Now you don't!"

"Wow! I could really use something like that!" Robert reaches for the cape. He grabs it off your shoulders.

"It's my cape!" you shout, hanging on to it. "I found it."

"The cape is big—let's cut it in half," Robert says. "You can wear half, and I'll wear half."

If you say okay to cutting the cape,
turn to page 6.

If you say you won't cut the cape in half,
turn to page 30.

Todd races toward first base. You pull your **13** cape tightly around you and run even faster than he does.

The fielder picks up the ball and throws it to first. But you're there to knock the ball aside! Then you roll the ball toward home plate.

"What's going on?" the first baseman yells.

Todd rounds first, then second, and heads for third. The catcher scoops up the ball to throw it to third base.

Turn to page 29.

14   You can come back later for Mr. Walters's apples. Right now you want to get to the game! You jog down the sidewalk to the vacant lot.

Your friend Todd is at bat. You know he's not a very good hitter. Some of the kids are teasing him. "Easy out!" they shout. "Two strikes. Why don't you just quit now?"

Todd ignores them and taps the plate with **15** his bat. The pitcher winds up . . .

You dash over to Todd. As the pitcher throws, you leap in front of the plate. Even before Todd can swing, you grab the ball and fling it into left field.

Turn to page 24.

You decide to pick some of those apples from Mr. Walters's tree. Mr. Walters is looking out of his living room window. You stick out your tongue at him. You're feeling pretty brave because you're invisible!

You hope Butch is sleeping, or out back somewhere. You're about to climb the tree when you smell something yummy! You creep over to the house and peek through the kitchen door. On the table inside are two apple pies, still steaming from the oven.

If there's anything you like better than shiny red apples, it's hot apple pie! And Mr. Walters and his wife don't need *two* of them!

Should you take a pie? Or stick to fresh apples and climb the tree?

If you take a pie, turn to page 27.

If you climb the tree, turn to page 25.

18   You hear other people shouting, too. Whatever's going on, enough people are already there to help. You decide to stay at the game.

Robert's sister Carol Ann is batting next. Carol Ann almost always hits the ball, but it never goes very far. You stand near the shortstop and wait.

The pitcher lobs the ball across the plate. Carol Ann swings. "Strike one!" The pitcher throws another. "Strike two!" The pitcher winds up and throws a fast ball. Carol Ann hits it right between you and the shortstop!

Is the shortstop going to scoop up the ball? No way—not if you have anything to do with it! You kick the rolling ball hard, way into left field. Carol Ann makes it to third!

You play invisible baseball all afternoon. Thanks to you, Todd gets another home run, and Carol Ann scores twice.

When the sun dips behind the trees, the game breaks up at last.

Turn to page 46.

You grope around until you find Robert, lift the cape, and quickly slip underneath it. Now you're both invisible.

"You're going to mess everything up," Robert whispers. He gives you a shove. You fall over backward—the whole cape goes with you! It slips off Robert and covers you as you hit the ground.

You look up just as Larry steps outside. He can't see *you,* but he can sure see Robert.

"What do you think you're doing with those water balloons?" Larry growls at Robert.

"Uh . . . er . . ." is all Robert can say. He's so scared that he drops the balloons. They burst and splatter water on his feet!

"Way to go!" Larry sneers. "You're all wet, *Bob!*" He starts forward, his fists up. You're afraid he'll punch Robert out! You have to do something fast!

Turn to page 28.

22   You decide not to tell Robert about the cape yet. You want to try it out first.

You hold your breath and tiptoe around Robert. You're only inches away from him, but he can't see you. You creep down the stairs and out the door.

As soon as you're outside, you hear, "Batter up!" Some of the kids must be playing in the vacant lot down the street. Invisible baseball could be fun, you think, as you hurry down the sidewalk.

You pass Mr. Walters's house. Mr. Walters has the biggest apple tree in town. Mr. Walters also hates kids, and so does his boxer, Butch.

You stare up at all the shiny red fruit. Your mouth is watering. Should you pick some apples? After all, you're invisible. Or are you going to go straight to the baseball game?

If you stop to pick apples, turn to page 17.

If you go straight to the baseball game, turn to page 14.

24   "Todd swung so fast, I didn't even see the bat move!" the pitcher mumbles.

But Todd is so surprised that he freezes.

"Run, dummy!" you yell, forgetting for a second that you're invisible!

Turn to page 13.

You jump up and grab the lowest branch of **25**
the apple tree with both hands. You're just
pulling yourself up when one of your hands
slips!

You almost fall! "Oooooops!" you cry out.

Mr. Walters and Butch hear you! They rush
out of the house. "Who's in my apple tree?"
Mr. Walters shouts. He stands under the tree,
peering up into the branches. He can't see
you. But as you scramble higher, you knock
some apples down. They drop one by one
onto Mr. Walters and Butch.

Turn to page 36.

Those pies look too good to pass up! **27**
There's no one in the kichen. Anyway, you're invisible, right?

The screen door creaks a little when you open it. You tiptoe to the kitchen table. The pie is still steaming. You break off a piece of crust and pop it in your mouth.

It's as yummy as it looks! You grab a spoon and dig into the filling. It's spicy and delicious. But you've only had a few mouthfuls when you're interrupted by a long, low growl. It's *Butch!*

You stand still as a statue, barely breathing.

Turn to page 34.

28   You jump to your feet. Still wrapped in the cape, you circle Larry. When you're behind him, you take the cape off.

"Hey, fatso!" you yell.

While Larry is charging at you, Robert dashes out the front gate. You slip the cape back on and dash to the end of the yard.

Larry spins around until he's dizzy, trying to find you. "Where are you, you little worm?" he shouts.

"Right here, creepo!" you call out, pulling the cape off again.

Turn to page 44.

"Hey, catcher—over here!" you shriek from first base.

The catcher whirls in your direction. She's so confused she drops the ball! Then she throws it to third base. But it flies over the third baseman's head. And Todd's on his way home!

"Todd hit a home run!" his teammates shout.

You hear someone else shouting, too, not far down the street. "Help—police! Stop him!"

Should you find out what's happening? Or do you stay where you are?

If you decide to find out what's happening, turn to page 4.

If you stay at the game, turn to page 18.

"I don't want to cut the cape in half," you tell Robert. "What if it won't work anymore?"

"Let's take turns, then," Robert says. "Me first, because I'm your guest." He grabs the cape and whips it on. You hear him clattering down the stairs.

"Let's wear it together!" you shout after Robert.

"No—I want to get even with Larry!" Robert answers. "You'd be in the way!"

"Are you nuts?" you yell, running downstairs, too. "Larry is the biggest bully in school!"

"I'm invisible, remember?" says Robert's voice.

You hear him walk down the hall and follow him into the kitchen. You watch his jacket rise in the air. Several empty balloons seem to float from a pocket toward the kitchen sink.

You can't see Robert. But the balloons swell under the water faucet until they're ready to burst!

Turn to page 38.

You get down on your hands and knees on the sidewalk to trip Larry as he runs by. Since you're invisible, he should tumble right over you. You push the hood of your cape back to see better, and Larry suddenly skids to a stop.

"Aaaah!" he screams. His face turns deathly pale. "No—keep away from me!"

What's the matter with him? you wonder.

Larry whirls around and dashes toward Mr. Brown. "Help! Help!"

Now they'll catch him! you say to yourself.

Turn to page 41.

34 Butch pads toward the table, his fangs bared.

As long as I don't move, I'm okay, you tell yourself.

But even though Butch can't see you or hear you . . . he can *smell* you! With a snarl, he leaps on you, his teeth snapping shut on your cape. You try to pull it away from him, but Butch won't let go. You hear footsteps hurrying toward you—it's Mr. Walters! Now you're done for. . . .

"Stop that! Have you gone crazy?" Mr. Walters yells at the dog. You jerk the cape and make sure you're covered and still invisible.

"You ate the pie, too!" Mr. Walters says to Butch. He grabs Butch's collar and drags him away from you, still snapping. "Bad dog— you're going without dinner!"

As you spoon up more pie, you feel sorry for Butch—but only a little.

The End

Butch yelps, and Mr. Walters jumps out of the way. "There's something very funny going on here!" Mr. Walters says angrily. "And I'm not moving until I find out what it is!"

Butch growls. He's not moving, either!

It's a good thing you like apples, because you may be in this tree for an awfully long time!

The End

38   The bulging balloons disappear under the cape that Robert is wearing.

You see the door swing open and hear Robert cross the porch. Then you listen to his footsteps thump on the sidewalk. You follow the sounds of his feet right up to the front steps of Larry's house.

"Hey, Larry!" Robert's voice yells. "Get out here, you creep!"

Uh-oh . . . When Larry opens the door, he won't see Robert—he'll see *you*, standing by yourself on his front lawn. And he'll think *you* called him a creep!

There's no time to run away. You've got to find a place to hide, and fast! Do you jump under the cape with Robert . . . or behind a big bush near the street?

If you hide under the cape with Robert, turn to page 21.

If you dart behind the bush, turn to page 10.

But Mr. Brown runs away, too. "I s-see it **41** but I d-don't believe it!" he stammers. "It's horrible!"

What's horrible? You look all around, but you don't see a thing!

"Eeeek!" *Thump!* Mrs. Willis faints right onto the sidewalk.

Then you hear Fred, the barber, yell, "A floating head!" He races into his shop, slams the door, and locks it!

A floating head?

As you scramble to your feet, you catch sight of something in the glass of a store window. You pushed only the hood of your cape back, so most of you is still invisible . . . *except for your head!* The floating head is *yours!*

The End

You continue to follow Robert down the street. He obviously thinks he's invisible. He doesn't know that half a cape works only half as well!

You follow him to the movie theater. The swinging doors seem to open by themselves as Robert sneaks past the ticket lady. You run in right behind him.

He's totally invisible in the brightly lit lobby. You watch as a box of popcorn rises into the air and disappears under Robert's half of the cape. Then the inside door opens. You follow Robert into the dark theater.

Now the usher can see Robert as clearly in the dark room as you can. "Hold it just a minute!" he growls. "Where is your ticket stub?"

Turn to page 8.

44   Larry runs straight at you. You put the cape on at the last minute and step aside. *Whooops!* Larry falls over a lawn chair!

You could keep this up all afternoon! You race to the side yard, ready to yell something even nastier. And that's when you realize . . . you're not wearing your cape! It must have fallen off!

You're *visible* . . . and here comes Larry!

The End

46 You want to talk to Todd and Carol Ann. But you don't want to scare them. You duck behind a tree, take off your cape, and fold it up.

"Hey, Todd! Carol Ann! Wait for me!" you shout.

They turn around. "Who said that?" Todd asks.

Carol Ann shakes her head. "I don't *see* anybody."

They *must see* you—they're staring right at you! Then you look down at yourself . . . and you don't see anything, either! You're not wearing the cape, but you're still invisible!

"Oh, no!" you cry. "Something's very wrong!"

Turn to page 53.

You don't have to wait long to find out—
he's waiting on the school steps on Monday morning.

You take a deep breath. "Hi, Larry," you say bravely.

"Hi" must sound like *hai* to Larry. In a flash, he's off the steps and inside the building. He'll never mess with the Karate Kid again!

The End

50   You decide to try and scare Larry by barking. You make sounds like your grandmother's German shepherd when he's angry: "RRRRUFFFF! RRRRUFFFF!"

Larry slows down a little when he hears the barks.

"ROOOOOW! ROOOOOW!" You howl like the cranky husky on your street.

Larry stops running and looks around nervously.

Now you growl like Mr. Walters's mean old boxer, Butch. "GRRROWWW! GRRROWWW!"

It works! Larry makes a U-turn and dashes straight into Mr. Brown's powerful arms!

You growl once more, just for fun . . . and hear an echo right behind you. It's the *real* Butch. He may not be able to see you, but he can still *smell* you!

The End

52   Larry lunges at you.

"Hai!" you shout, pretending you know karate. You kick the air with one foot . . . and Larry falls to the ground!

"Hey—cut that out!" Larry says, slowly getting to his feet.

You know you didn't touch him. But you have a good idea who did!

"Hai!" You do another karate kick. Larry stumbles sideways.

"Stop it!" Larry whines.

"Hai!" you shout again . . . and Larry runs back into his house and slams the door behind him.

"We did it! We did it!" Robert yells from somewhere in front of you.

You're glad Robert came to your rescue just now, but what happens next time you see Larry?

Turn to page 49.

That's when you spot a blue tag sewn onto the cape. In small print, it says, WARNING: FADING WILL OCCUR WITH OVERUSE.

Only it's not the cape that has faded—it's *you!*

The End

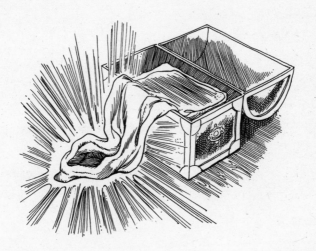

ABOUT THE AUTHOR

Susan Saunders grew up on a ranch in Texas, where she learned rodeo riding. A graduate of Barnard College, she has been a ceramicist and an editor of filmstrips for children. She is the author of *Wales' Tale* and *Charles Rat's Picnic,* both Junior Literary Guild selections, and *The Green Slime, Runaway Spaceship, Attack of the Monster Plants, The Miss Liberty Caper, Haunted Halloween Party, The Movie Mystery,* and *Light on Burro Mountain* in the Bantam Skylark Choose Your Own Adventure series. Ms. Saunders is also the author of *Mystery Cat,* available from Bantam Skylark Books.

ABOUT THE ILLUSTRATOR

Ron Wing is a cartoonist and illustrator who has contributed work to many publications. For the past several years, he has illustrated the Bantam humor series, *Larry Wilde's Official Joke Books.* In addition, he has illustrated *Search for the Mountain Gorillas, You Are a Shark, Forest of Fear, Terror Island,* and *The Mardi Gras Mystery* in Bantam's Choose Your Own Adventure series and *Haunted Halloween Party* in the Skylark Choose Your Own Adventure series. Mr. Wing now lives and works in Benton, Pennsylvania.